Picnic Surprise

Written and illustrated by
Jenny Neal

Dedications

To Emily, your love of books motivates me to write and draw.

Charlotte, your mischievousness has brought bundles of inspiration.

Daddy and I love you both dearly!

Special thanks to my editor Stacy Bax

Text and Illustrations Copyright © Jenny Neal of The Kilns Creative Ltd 2021

The moral rights of Jenny Neal of The Kilns Creative Ltd to be identified as the author and illustrator of this work, have been asserted in accordance with the Copyright, Designs and Patents Act 1988. All rights reserved.

ISBN: 9798771688138

contains something super yummy
Thank you
Chilham St. Mary's Church of England Primary School for helping with the ABC feature at the back of this book.
DO NOT OPEN!

Tucked away in their make-shift den,
planning a special tea.

Two girls are labelling and learning,
Brit prancing around with glee.

TEACHER BRIT
MY NEW FOUND NAME,

TEACHING AMY
IS THE GREATEST GAME!

ABC's, they're NOT just for school,

labelling and learning is SO COOL!

'a' is for **apple** this ones red,
juicy and **fat!**

'b' is for **banana**
Oh Amy don't do that!

banana

SPLAT

We need **carrots** and **cucumber** sticks that are scrummy with a dip.

C

carrot
cucumber

'd' is for **drinks,**
we all need something to sip.

'g' is for **gerkin** and 'h' is for **ham**,
we must have these in sandwiches
for **Stan** and **Soppy Sam**.

I LOVE strawberry **ice cream**, we'll have this for 'i'

i ice cream

and 'j' is for **jelly**,
ideal for Captain Spy.

'k' is for **kiwi**, our fruit salad
is near complete,

'l' can be for **lemonade**,

SHHHH!

IT'S OUR
NAUGHTY
LITTLE TREAT!

Now, we need a **melon** for Helen
and **nuggets** for...

AMY.
DON'T.
SUCK.
IT!!!

m
melon

n
nuggets

o
oranges

'o' is for **oranges** lets store them in this **bucket**.

'p' is for **pizza**
daddy's ones are THE BEST!

'r' is for **raisins**, chew carefully,
I don't want you to choke!

'**t**' is for **tomatoes**,
perfect with cubes of cheese.

'U' is for **unsalted nuts**,
share them out carefully **please.**

'v' is for **vegetables**,
I think we have plenty of those!

'**w**' is for **waffles**,
AMY! DON'T STICK IT UP YOUR NOSE!

'X' is for **eXtra large box**, containing an exciting surprise for dear old Mr Fox.

'y' is for **yum-yums**,
these twisted donuts are so scrummy.

We're nearly done, this has been fun!

Labelling food makes one hungry tummy!

and finally
'Z' is for **zillions of candles,**
although he's ONLY forty four.

The ABC party is ready,

I CAN'T WAIT ANYMORE!!

BURP!

NO MORE!
My tummy is too sore!

THANK YOU

Chilham, St. Mary's
Church of England
Primary School.

Your artistic touch to this
book wows me!

J.N

'a' is for
apricot
by James

'b' is for
burger
by Bonnie

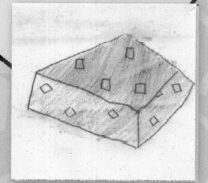

'c' is for
chocolate brownie
by Charlotte

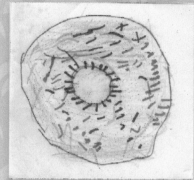

'd' is for
donut
by Eligh

'e' is for
edam cheese
by Eden

'f' is for
fish and chips
by Christina

'g' is for
gooseberries
by Sasha

'h' is for
honey
by Mia

**'i' is for
ice cream**
by Bluebell

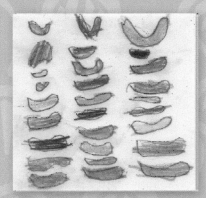

**'j' is for
jelly beans**
by Jessie

**'k' is for
kiwi**
by Aida

**'l' is for
lemon**
by Fred

**'m' is for
marshmellow**
by Holly

**'n' is for
nuggets and noodles**
by Isla

**'o' is for
olives**
by Olive

**'p' is for
pineapple**
by Josh

**'q' is for
quarter pounder with cheese**
by Jamie

'r' is for
raspberry cupcake
by Lucy

's' is for
strawberry
by Phoebe

't' is for
tomato
by Bobby

'u' is for
ugli / uniq fruit
by Poppy

'v' is for
vanilla ice cream
by Dillon

'w' is for
wedge - potato wedge
by Nat

'x' is for
x-ray tetra fish sandwich
by Emily

'y' is for
yoghurt
by Iona

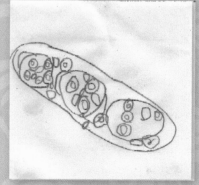

'z' is for
zapiekanka
by Finn

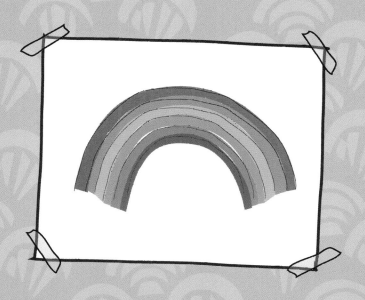

Created in the winter lockdown 2020

PST!. is there more cake?

Also available:

'Stick it Brit' is a children's rhyming book
dedicated to encourage fun home learning,
supporting children's memory through repetition.

" WRITE IT, POST IT, SEE IT, LEARN IT, THEN STICK!" SHE WOULD SAY."

"This will help me pass my test! Hip hip hooray!"

Where would your little one's place their sticky notes??

Printed in Great Britain
by Amazon